# Five reaso...
## love Isad...... .....n . . .

Meet the magical,
fang-tastic Isadora Moon!

Isadora's cuddly toy, Pink Rabbit,
has been magicked to life!

What's your favourite
kind of birthday party?

Isadora's family is crazy!

Enchanting
pink and black
pictures

# What's your favourite kind of birthday party?

There were lots of hula hoops and assault courses at my favourite birthday party.
– Frankie

Mine had a pirate theme, it was brilliant. I had a parrot! (Not a real one.)
– Charlie

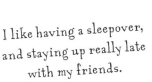

I like having a sleepover,
and staying up really late
with my friends.
– Ava

Any birthday party,
as long as it's not for boys!
– Harriet

Parties where you play
musical bumps are the best.
– Lex

My dad took me to the cinema
with my best friend last year,
that was my best birthday.
– Sammy

# Family Tree

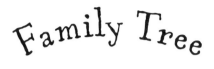

My Mum
Countess Cordelia
Moon

Baby Honeyblossom

My Dad
Count Bartholomew
Moon

Me!
Isadora Moon

Pink Rabbit

For vampires, fairies and humans everywhere!

And for Georgina, my favourite sister.

# OXFORD
**UNIVERSITY PRESS**

Great Clarendon Street, Oxford OX2 6DP

Oxford University Press is a department of the University of Oxford.
It furthers the University's objective of excellence in research, scholarship, and
education by publishing worldwide. Oxford is a registered trade mark of Oxford
University Press in the UK and in certain other countries

First published 2016

British Library Cataloguing in Publication Data

Data available

ISBN: 978-0-19-274435-7

10

Printed in China

Paper used in the production of this book is a natural,
recyclable product made from wood grown in sustainable forests.
The manufacturing process conforms to the environmental
regulations of the country of origin.

# ISADORA ★ MOON

## Has a Birthday

# Harriet Muncaster

OXFORD
UNIVERSITY PRESS

# Chapter ONE

Isadora Moon, that's me! And this is Pink Rabbit. He was my favourite stuffed toy but my Mum magicked him alive with her wand. He comes everywhere with me, even to birthday parties!

I have been to lots of birthday parties since I started school. Human ones! They are very interesting and very different from the parties we have at home. I had only ever been to vampire or fairy ones before I met my human friends. That's because my mum is a fairy and my dad is a vampire. Yes, really!

Do you know what that makes me?

A vampire fairy!

I am a bit of both. I wasn't sure where I fitted in but then I went to human school and discovered that everyone is a little bit different and that's the best way to be.

I have especially enjoyed going to all my friends' human birthday parties. They are all so different! I couldn't wait for my own birthday so that I could have a party of my own.

'I hope you will be having a nice traditional vampire party when it's your birthday,' said Dad.

'Hmm,' I said.

I wasn't sure about having a vampire party. I think my friends would find it a bit scary. A vampire party is always held in the dead of night and you have to dress very smartly and have very neat hair. Vampires are very fussy about their appearance. They like to play flying games, and shoot across the sky at lightning-quick speed. My wings can never keep up as they are more flappy, like fairy wings. Vampires also like to eat red food at their parties and drink red juice. I hate all red food.

'How about a nice traditional fairy one?' suggested Mum. 'That would be lovely!'

I remembered the fairy party Mum organized for me when I was four. It was a swimming party. Fairies love nature so we went to a wild forest stream. It was very cold and there were lots of weeds and fish in the water.

'It's so invigorating!' Mum cried as she jumped into the water with all the fairy guests.

I stood and shivered in the water. Pink Rabbit sat on a rock. He hates getting wet.

'I'd rather have a human party like my friends at school,' I told Mum and Dad honestly. 'They are much more fun.'

'Impossible,' said Dad. 'There's nothing more fun than a vampire party. Think of all the delicious red food!'

'I think another swimming party would be wonderful,' said Mum dreamily. 'We could have a campfire afterwards and make flower crowns.'

'I really would like a human one,' I said. 'Please? At a human one there are all sorts of fun things!'

'What sort of fun things?' asked Mum suspiciously.

'Well, at Zoe's party last week we all

had to wear costumes. It was called fancy dress.'

'I wondered why you were wearing those pink bunny ears,' said Dad.

'I was being Pink Rabbit!' I told him. 'And Pink Rabbit dressed up as me. It was so much fun. We had cake and ice cream and party bags and we played pass the parcel.'

'Pass the what?' said Mum.

'The parcel!' I said. 'It goes round and round in a circle and at the end there's a surprise!'

'Sounds very odd,' said Mum. 'And what is a party bag?'

'It's a little bag you give the guests at the end of the party,' I explained. 'It's full of little presents and also a slice of the birthday cake wrapped in a tissue.'

'I didn't know humans ate tissues,' said Dad.

'The week before, it was Oliver's birthday,' I continued. 'He had a bouncy castle at his party, and a magician.'

'A magician sounds good,' said Mum, perking up.

'A pretend one,' I said quickly. 'He didn't do real magic like you can do with your wand.'

Mum looked very confused. 'Why not?' she asked.

I shrugged. 'It's just the way they do it at human parties.'

'It all sounds very peculiar,' said Dad.

'I really would love a human birthday party,' I said, smiling my most angelic smile.

Mum and Dad sighed.

'Well . . . all right then,' said Mum.

'I suppose we could try a human

birthday party this year,' agreed Dad.

Pink Rabbit and I jumped up and down in excitement.

'Thank you! Thank you!' I shouted. Pink Rabbit can't shout but he waved his paws in the air gleefully.

When the time came to start planning my birthday party Mum and Dad seemed to be very organized.

'Leave it to us,' they said. 'We don't need any help.'

'Are you sure you know what you're doing?' I asked nervously.

'Oh yes!' said Dad. 'We've got all the ideas written down: pass the parcel, magician, cake, balloons, presents, bouncy castle, fancy dress, party bags . . .'

'It's going to be the best birthday party ever!' said Mum.

'There need to be invitations,' I told them. 'Don't forget the invitations.'

Dad frowned and scratched his head. Then he wrote 'invitations' at the bottom of the list.

The next day at school we were in
a maths lesson when suddenly there came
a great flapping sound from outside.

'What on earth is that?' said Miss
Cherry, darting towards the window.

A swarm of envelopes were flying through the air on little bat wings and now they were tapping against the windows trying to get in. 'Oh my goodness!' Miss Cherry exclaimed.

I felt my face go red with embarrassment.

'Let them in!' cried Oliver. 'Let's see what they are!'

'Don't let them in!' wailed shy Samantha, ducking down behind her desk.

The envelopes kept beating their wings against the glass until one of them found an open window. It beckoned to all the others. Then they all came flying in, fluttering and flapping, landing one by one on my friends' desks.

'It's an invitation!'
cried Oliver, once he had ripped
his envelope open.

'A birthday party!' yelled Zoe.
'At Isadora's house!'

'It's fancy dress!' shouted someone
else. 'I love fancy dress!'

All the children were chattering
excitedly now but Miss Cherry did not
look too pleased. Now she had got over
her surprise she seemed just a tiny bit
annoyed.

'Isadora,' she said. 'It's not really
the done thing to make such a scene in
the middle of a lesson.'

I slunk down in my chair feeling like
I wanted to disappear.

'Sorry,' I whispered.

DEAR: Oliver

You're invited to Isadora
Moon's Birthday Party!

WHEN: This Saturday

WHERE: The big pink
and black house

TIME: 10AM ~ 3PM

RSVP

PS Please wear fancy dress!

When I got home that afternoon, I marched into the kitchen where Mum and Dad were busy making party decorations.

'You got me into trouble at school sending those bat invitations,' I told them.

Dad looked surprised.

'But they were marvellous,' he said. 'Did you see how I used my very best handwriting?'

'Did your friends like them?' asked Mum.

'Well, yes . . .' I said. 'But they weren't proper human party invitations, you know.'

'Weren't they?' asked Mum.

'No!' I said. 'With human invitations

you just hand them out yourself. They don't have *wings.*'

'How boring,' said Dad who was in the middle of sticking stars on to a 'HAPPY BIRTHDAY' banner.

Happy Birthday

'You *are* planning a human birthday party, aren't you?' I asked worriedly.

'Yes,' said Dad. 'Don't worry, Isadora. We have it all under control.' He tapped his list of ideas. 'We are following your instructions exactly.'

I peered again at the list. 'Pass the parcel, magician, cake, balloons, presents, bouncy castle, fancy dress, party bags.' Invitations could now be crossed out.

'OK,' I said, feeling reassured once again. 'But you know you don't have to include all those things in the party. Most human parties just have one or two of those things.'

'Of course,' said Dad absent-mindedly.

I made myself a peanut butter sandwich and made my way upstairs to my turret bedroom.

# Chapter TWO

On the morning of my birthday I woke
up bright and early. The sun was shining
outside and the birds were chirping.
I poked Pink Rabbit awake.

'Today's the day!' I said to him.
I leapt out of bed and we flew down
the stairs together.

Mum, Dad, and my baby sister,

Honeyblossom, were all in the kitchen waiting for me. The table had been laid for breakfast and there was a pink package sitting in front of my place all tied up with glittery ribbon.

'Happy Birthday, Isadora!' cried Mum and Dad together. They both sat at the table smiling. Mum had a bowl of flower nectar yoghurt with wild berries in front of her and Dad had already started drinking his red juice. Vampires love red juice. Honeyblossom was sitting in her high chair and happily waving her bottle of pink milk in the air.

I sat down at the table.

'Can I open my present?' I asked excitedly.

'Of course!' said Mum. 'You've only got one because it's a very, very special one this year.'

I reached for the present. I was

just about to pick it up and tear off the wrapping when . . .

DING DONG!

Mum swooped the present away from under my hands and jumped to her feet.

'Must be Cousin Wilbur!' she said. 'He's arrived early. We mustn't let him see Isadora's present. He'll be very jealous.'

She put my present in the cupboard under the sink and hurried to answer the door.

'You'll have to open it later,' said Dad, sounding a bit disappointed.

Cousin Wilbur came into the room. He was wearing a long black robe with silver stars on it and a pointy hat on his head.

Wilbur is a wizard. Well, almost a wizard.
He is a wizard-in-training and also a
bossy know-it-all. He thinks he knows
everything because he is older than me.

'Happy Birthday, Isadora,' he said.

Then he puffed out his chest and stuck his nose in the air in a smug sort of way.

'I am your birthday magician,' he explained. 'Wilbur the Great!'

'But . . .' I began.

'I have some excellent tricks up my sleeve,' Wilbur continued. 'Your friends will all be very impressed.'

'It's very kind of you to come and help out at Isadora's party,' said Mum.

'It is, isn't it,' agreed Wilbur.

I frowned. 'Wilbur is a real magician,' I said. 'The magician is only supposed to do pretend magic.'

Mum, Dad, and Wilbur all looked confused.

'Well that's just silly,' snorted Wilbur. 'Can a human magician do this?'

He took his hat off and held it in front of him. Then he said a very long and complicated word and stuck his hand into the hat . . .

'ARGHHHH!' he screamed. 'Get it OFF!!'

From the end of Wilbur's finger, holding on by its teeth, dangled a large white rabbit. Wilbur began to swing his arm around and around.

'GET IT OFF!' he screamed.

Pink Rabbit put his paws over his eyes and Honeyblossom started to cry. Mum picked up her wand from the

breakfast table and waved it. The white
rabbit vanished into thin air.

Wilbur continued to swing his arm around and scream for a while longer before realizing the rabbit had disappeared. Wilbur's face went bright red—as red as his sore finger.

'Ahem,' he said. 'I might have to practise that trick.'

'Yes, that might be a good idea,' said Dad hurriedly. 'Why don't you go and do a little bit of practice before the guests arrive?'

'It won't be long now,' said Mum, looking at the clock. 'There's a lot to fit in today so we asked everyone to arrive early. Isadora, you had better go and change into your fancy-dress costume!'

I felt butterflies of excitement
flutter in my stomach. It was almost
time for my party! I grabbed Pink Rabbit's
paw and we ran upstairs to change. As
I put my costume on, I started to feel a
tiny bit nervous. Would my friends think
my family were too weird? None of them
had met Mum and Dad properly before.
And what would they think of Cousin
Wilbur? I hoped he wasn't going to be
a show-off today.

'Bewitching!' said Dad when I came
downstairs in my costume. 'You look just
like a bat!'

I was very pleased with my outfit. Dad
had helped me to make it the night before.

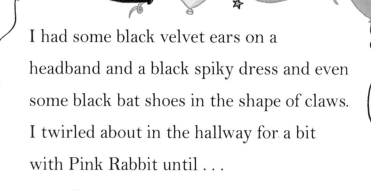

I had some black velvet ears on a headband and a black spiky dress and even some black bat shoes in the shape of claws. I twirled about in the hallway for a bit with Pink Rabbit until . . .

DING DONG!

The first guest had arrived! It was Zoe. She was wearing a black catsuit and standing on the doorstep with her mum.

'Happy Birthday, Isadora!' she said, handing me a parcel wrapped up with a big pink bow.

'Thank you, Zoe!' I said, suddenly

feeling so happy I could burst.

Zoe's mum peered curiously into the

hallway.

'I see your parents have dressed up too, Isadora,' she said. 'What fun! That's a lovely fairy costume your mum is wearing. The wings look so realistic! And what a great job they've done decorating the house! The bat chandelier is a nice touch for the party.'

'It's not just for the party . . .' I started to explain, but Zoe's mum was looking at her watch.

'I must be off,' she said. 'I'll be back to pick you up later, Zoe!' She gave Zoe a quick kiss on the cheek and hurried away down the garden path.

Oliver was next to arrive. He was dressed as a vampire.

'Wonderful!' said Dad when he saw Oliver's costume. 'I didn't know you had invited any vampires, Isadora!'

'He's not a real . . .' I began.

'I had better get some red juice for the vampire,' said Dad, hurrying towards the fridge.

The doorbell went again and Mum opened it. Shy Samantha stood on the doorstep dressed as a fairy.

'Oooh!' squeaked Mum. 'I didn't realize you had invited any fairies, Isadora! How wonderful. We can have lots of chats about nature!' She took Samantha's hand and led her into the kitchen.

When all my friends had arrived, we went into the great hall. Mum and Dad had done a great job decorating it. Silver stars hung from the ceiling and there were pink and black balloons all over the floor. All my friends seemed very impressed.

Some of them were running round the room and playing with the balloons. They all seemed happy.

*Maybe my party will be fun, just like a human one after all!* I thought.

# Chapter THREE

'Time for pass the parcel!' boomed
Dad, who had put on a pair of snazzy
sunglasses to protect his eyes from
the morning light. It was still very
early for him to be awake. Vampires
usually sleep through the day. 'You all
know the rules, don't you?' he shouted.
'Of course you do, you're humans!'

Then he produced a big parcel from behind his back.

'Everyone in a circle, please!' he said.

My friends and I shuffled ourselves into a circle on the floor and Dad gave the parcel to one of the children.

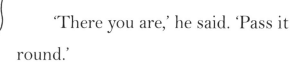

'There you are,' he said. 'Pass it round.'

We all started to pass the parcel round the circle. But something was missing.

'Music!' I whispered to Dad. 'We need music!'

'Music!' shouted Dad to Mum.

Mum opened her mouth and started to sing a tinkly fairy song. I felt my face go red with embarrassment. Some of my friends started to giggle.

'That's right!' called Dad. 'Pass it round. Round and round it goes!'

The parcel went round and round the circle. And round and round again! I started to wonder when Mum was going to stop singing. I was about to whisper to Dad again when suddenly there was an almighty bang.

'SURPRISE!!' shouted Dad as the parcel exploded in Oliver's hands. Fireworks shot out of it and up into the air.

Glittery pink sparks and sparkling fizzing stars swirled and whirled around the room.

'Oh no!' I said to Pink Rabbit.

But my friends didn't seem to mind.
In fact, they seemed to like it. They all
stood up and started dancing to Mum's
song under the falling sparks.

'They're so pretty!' breathed Zoe
as she tried to catch a shooting star.

'It's magical!' yelled Sashi.

Everyone danced until the sparks
stopped falling and Mum stopped singing.

'Time for the magician,' announced
Dad, opening the door for Wilbur.
He swept in, swishing his starry robe.

'It's Wilbur the Great, actually,'
corrected Wilbur. 'Sit down everyone,'
he said bossily. 'Today I am going to show

you a wonderful trick. Who wants to be turned into a box of frogs?'

I groaned. A boy from my class called Bruno put his hand in the air and Wilbur gestured for Bruno to come and stand at the front.

Wilbur rolled up his sleeves,
closed his eyes, and puffed out his chest
importantly. Then he pointed his finger
at Bruno.

'Allikazambanana!!' he said.

There was a loud BANG and a puff
of pink smoke.

Bruno disappeared and in his place
stood a large cardboard box. There were
loud croaking sounds coming from inside.

'WOW!' said all my friends.
'AMAZING!'

'It's like real magic!'
said Oliver.

We all watched
as the frogs started

to jump out of the
box. Wilbur looked
very pleased with himself.

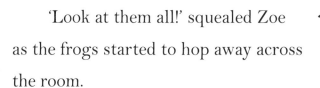

'Look at them all!' squealed Zoe
as the frogs started to hop away across
the room.

'Eww,' said Samantha, 'I hate
slimy frogs.'

'What next?' asked
Wilbur. 'Who wants to
see me pull a rabbit from
my hat?'

Everyone cheered,
except Pink Rabbit who looked
very worried.

Wilbur put on some thick gloves.

'Just in case it bites,' he said winking, and everyone laughed.

'Wilbur,' I called out worriedly. 'What about Bruno?'

'What about him?' said Wilbur, starting to put his gloved hand into his hat.

'Shouldn't you turn him back now?' I asked.

Wilbur looked surprised.

'Oh,' he said. 'Well, yes. I suppose I should.'

He took his hand out of his hat, holding a white fluffy rat.

'That's not a rabbit!' shouted Oliver laughing. 'That's a rat!' All my friends

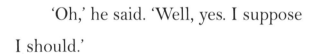

were laughing now. They thought Wilbur
was hilarious.

'Oh,' said Wilbur, disappointed.
'So it is.'

'WILBUR!'

I shouted. 'You need to turn Bruno back into a boy.'

'All right,' said Wilbur looking annoyed. 'You'll all have to catch the frogs though. If you forget one then Bruno might come back missing an ear or something.'

My friends and I went off in search of the frogs.

'We can't send Bruno home with only one ear!' I wailed.

'Let me help!' said Mum, holding her wand up in the air. But Wilbur did not want any help.

'No no,' he said. 'I can do it!'

At last all the frogs were collected and back in the box. We all stared expectantly at Wilbur. He seemed a little nervous.

'Don't everyone stare at me,' he ordered. 'It puts me off.'

Wilbur turned around so that he had his back to everyone and waved his arms about a bit. We all waited. There were a few loud bangs and a lot of smoke but eventually Bruno appeared.

'Ribbit,' he said.

'Oops! Hang on,' said Wilbur. He waved his hands again and said some more magic words.

Bruno blinked and looked confused,
but this time when he opened his mouth
words came out instead of croaks.

'That was awesome!' he said.

I breathed a sigh of relief.

'Thank goodness for that!' said Dad, swooping in. 'I think it's time for the next activity.'

'But I haven't finished my show, Uncle Bartholomew,' said Wilbur crossly.

'I think you have,' said Dad firmly. 'I think we will move on to the bouncy castle now.'

I felt my spirits rise. A bouncy castle! Surely nothing could go wrong with that. There was still time for my party to be like a proper human one.

# Chapter FOUR

We all followed Mum and Dad into the
back garden. Then Mum pointed her wand
at the sky. A silvery thread shot out of the
end and lassoed itself around one of the
fat fluffy clouds in the sky. Mum pulled it
down to the ground gently and pegged it
into the grass.

'Clouds make wonderful bouncy

castles,' she told everyone. 'So much softer and bouncier.'

I frowned. I should have known a human bouncy castle was too much to ask.

But my friends didn't seem to mind. They all looked astonished and excited. Their eyes were round like saucers.

'You can all hop on,' said Mum. 'Bounce away! Dad and I are going to go inside and put the candles on the birthday cake.'

Zoe was the first to take off her shoes
and jump on to the cloud.

'It's so soft!' she exclaimed as she
bounced up and down. 'I'm so high!'

Soon all my friends were on the cloud, bouncing around and laughing. It didn't look like anything could go wrong this time so I decided to join in. I took off my shoes and jumped up on to the cloud.

'Whee!' I cried.

Suddenly I felt very happy. Everyone was having a good time. Even Samantha!

It was just as much fun as a human party!

'It's like flying!' yelled Oliver.

As we soared higher and laughed and screamed, I noticed Wilbur come out of the house and into the garden. He walked over to the cloud and stared up at us.

'Do you want me to make it even bouncier?' he asked. 'Seeing as I didn't get to finish my show, I could do some more magic for you now.'

'Oh yes!' cried all my friends. 'Please do more magic!'

I stopped bouncing and jumped right off the cloud and on to the grass.

'I don't think that's a good idea, Wilbur—' I began.

'Why ever not?' said Wilbur. 'It will be much more fun if it's bouncier. Here, let me do some more magic.'

He rolled up his starry sleeves and waved his arms in the air.

'Kaboooooommmska!' he said and a shower of sparks shot out of his fingers.

The cloud gave a little wobble and my friends began to fly up higher and higher into the air.

'Wow!' Bruno cried. 'This is amazing! It IS bouncier! Look at me!'

'See?' said Wilbur. 'Much more fun!' He crossed his arms and looked down at me. 'You should just relax, Isadora,' he said.

But I couldn't relax. Something didn't seem right. The cloud was rocking and shaking. It couldn't handle the amount of bounce.

'Everyone get off!' I shouted in a panic as the cloud began to loosen from its pegs. But no one listened to me. They were all having too much fun. I tugged on Wilbur's sleeve.

'Look!' I said to him. 'It's about to fly away!'

'It's not going to fly away!' said Wilbur, rolling his eyes.

'It is!' I insisted, pointing at the pegs stuck into the grass. One by one they began to pop out of the ground and slowly the cloud began to rise up into the air.

'Oh,' said Wilbur, staring in horror. 'Whoops.'

'I told you!' I said crossly.

We watched as the cloud floated higher and higher.

'Do something!' I said to Wilbur.

'I can't bring a cloud down from the

sky!' said Wilbur. 'I won't be learning
how to do that until next term at
wizard school.'

'I'll get Mum. You stay here and don't
move!' I shouted.

I ran to the kitchen where Dad was putting the last few candles into an enormous cake.

'Whoa, Isadora, you're not supposed to see the cake yet!' he said.

'It's an emergency!' I told him. 'Where's Mum?'

'She had to pop upstairs for a minute,' said Dad. 'Honeyblossom was crying and needed some pink milk.'

'Oh no, oh no!' I wailed.

'What's wrong?' asked Dad.

I was going to explain when I saw the very thing I needed sitting on the kitchen table: Mum's wand. I grabbed it and ran back outside. Wilbur was still standing where I had left him, staring at the sky.

'There it is,' he said to me, pointing at a speck in the distance. It looked so small and so far away. There was no time to lose. I flapped my wings and rose up into the air.

I flew as fast as I could—faster than
ever before—but it still took a long time
to catch up with the cloud. At last I was
near enough to hear my friends' voices.
They had all stopped bouncing now. They
were sitting very still and looking very
scared. Some of them were lying on their

stomachs with their faces peering over the edge. Their eyes were big and round as they stared down at the ground miles and miles below. Pink Rabbit had his paws over his face.

'Isadora!' called Zoe as I landed gently on the cloud and sat down to get my breath back. 'We thought you were never coming!'

'We thought we were lost in the sky forever!' said Oliver.

Pink Rabbit just bounced over to me and put his paws round my legs.

'I'm sorry,' I said. 'It was my cousin, Wilbur. He should never have put more magic on the cloud.'

'But we're safe now you're here, aren't we?' asked Samantha.

I didn't feel very confident—I am only half fairy, and wand magic isn't my strong point—but I made myself smile

as though it was completely
normal to be stuck on top of a
cloud in the middle of the sky.

'Oh yes,' I said. 'Don't worry.
I'll find a way to get us down.
I've got my mum's wand.' I held
it up in the air and the pink star
glittered in the sunlight.

'Great!' said Oliver. 'We're saved!'

I felt nervous as I closed my eyes.
I wasn't sure if I could get the cloud and
all my friends back down to the ground
but I had to try.

I pictured the cloud in my mind's eye
floating gently back down to earth. Then
I waved the wand and opened my eyes.

Nothing happened.

*Oh dear*, I thought anxiously.

I closed my eyes to try again.

I concentrated on the cloud harder this time. I imagined it sinking down, down, down . . . I waved the wand as hard as I could.

But when I opened my eyes again, nothing had happened.

'Oh dear,' I said aloud.

'What is it?' asked Samantha in a small, scared voice.

'I'm not sure I can do it,' I said truthfully. 'This is big magic. I can only really do small bits of wand magic. And . . . and I don't always get my spells right.'

I remembered the time at Fairy School when I had tried to make a carrot cake appear but all I had managed was a carrot with bat wings that flew around the room and caused chaos.

'Oh dear,' said Samantha, sounding frightened. 'How will we ever get down?'

'We have to think of another way,'
said Zoe. 'There must be another way.'

Samantha screwed up her eyes as
though she were thinking very hard.
Then she opened them again and looked
a little less panicked.

'You know what my mum always
tells me,' she said. 'She says that
sometimes it's the small things that make
a difference. So maybe it will only take
a small bit of magic to get us out of this
big mess. We have to think of a spell you
CAN do!'

She pointed at the wings of her fairy
costume. 'Could you make these come
alive?' she asked.

I looked at the wings. They were only very small compared to the cloud.

'I can try,' I said.

Samantha looked around at all our friends sitting on the cloud in their fancy-dress costumes. She pointed at Bruno in his dragon suit.

'Do you think you could magic Bruno's dragon wings alive too?' she asked.

I looked at the two fabric wings sewn on to the back of Bruno's costume.

'Maybe!' I said, feeling excited. 'Yes, I think I could do that!'

'Well then, I have an idea,' said Samantha. 'Look how many of us have wings on our costumes. Bruno has dragon wings, I have fairy wings, Sashi has butterfly wings, Oliver has a cape, and, of course, you have real wings! If you could magic all the wings alive then half of us would be able to fly . . .'

'We could all help each other to fly back to my garden!' I said. 'Samantha, you're a genius!' I gave her a big hug and her face went as pink as Mum's hair.

'Let's try it,' I said.

We started with Bruno. I pointed Mum's wand at his little dragon wings and imagined them flapping to life.

At first it didn't work. The wings just
changed colour and then
went all spotty but
after a few tries
they gave a
little twitch and
flapped into life.
Bruno immediately
rose up into
the air.

'Wow!' he yelled.
'Look at me!'
I tried Samantha's fairy
wings next. It only took two
tries before they started to flap.

'Eeek!' squealed Samantha as she rose into the air.

'It's working!' shouted Zoe excitedly, though I could tell she was a little jealous that she had not chosen a costume with wings.

I had got the hang of the wand now and the last two spells were easy. Oliver and Sashi rose up into the air, shrieking with delight.

'OK, everyone,' I said. 'We all have to help each other now. The ones who can fly must hold hands with the ones who can't.'

I took Zoe's hand with one of mine and held on to Pink Rabbit's paw with the other. Soon all of us were floating up in the air.

'We must stick together,' I said to everyone.

'I'm scared!' said Samantha, looking fearfully down at the ground. It seemed

very far away. The houses and trees
looked tiny, like little models.

'Don't be frightened, Samantha,'
I reassured her. 'Flying is fun!'

'It *is* fun!' agreed Bruno. 'I wish
I could fly all the time!'

'I LOVE flying!' cried Oliver.

Together, we all flapped slowly
away from the cloud. There was nothing
beneath us now. Just air. Of course I am

used to that but my friends were not.

'EEEK!' squeaked Samantha.

'Whoa!' said Oliver.

I pointed at a pink-and-black speck
in the distance.

'Look,' I said, 'that's my house!
That's where we need to go. Follow me!'

I flew to the head of the group with
Zoe and Pink Rabbit. Flap, flap, flap went
my little bat wings.

'I can see our school,' said Zoe. 'And look, there's the park! It all looks very different from up here.'

'It's all so small!' said Sashi.

We were getting closer to my house now. I could just make out my turret bedroom window. In the garden there were three dots moving about. Mum, Dad, and Wilbur. They were waving their arms. Suddenly two of them shot up into the air and flew towards us.

'Oh my goodness,' said Mum when she reached us, 'we were so worried!'

'SO worried,' added Dad. 'We didn't know where the cloud had gone to.

By the time we came out into the garden
it had disappeared!'

'Disappeared completely!' said Mum.
'Oh, I'm so glad you're all safe.'

We all flew over the garden fence and
landed gently back on the grass.

'Wilbur explained what happened,'
said Dad, giving Wilbur a stern look.
'It was very brave of you to go and rescue
your friends, Isadora.'

'It wasn't just me,' I said. 'It was
Samantha. If it wasn't for her brilliant
idea we would still be stuck on the cloud.
Samantha really saved the day.'

'Well then,' said Mum. 'Thank you,
Samantha! Let's all give her three cheers!'

Everyone cheered for Samantha and
her face turned bright pink again. But
I could tell she was proud and pleased.

'It maybe wasn't the best idea to use
a cloud as a bouncy castle,' said Mum.
'I just got carried away. I'm sorry. I should
have just ordered a regular bouncy castle.
Next time I will.'

'NO!' shouted all my friends.

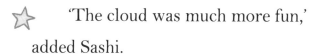 'The cloud was much more fun,'
added Sashi.

'We will try and be more normal
from now on,' said Dad. 'We can see this
party has been quite stressful for you,
Isadora.'

'NO!' shouted all my friends again.

'Please don't change,' pleaded Zoe.
'We love you and your family the way you
are, Isadora.'

'Yes, we do!' said Oliver. 'We love that your family is different.'

'Just keep being you!' said Bruno.

I looked around at everyone and felt a big smile spread over my face. I couldn't help it, I was just so happy! I even smiled at Cousin Wilbur.

'Really?' I said. 'You don't even mind that we got stuck on a cloud in the middle of the sky?'

'It was much more fun than a regular bouncy castle!' said Oliver.

'Though I am a bit hungry now,' said Bruno.

'Then it must be time for cake!' said Dad.

Chapter
FIVE

We all followed Dad back into
the house to the kitchen. A giant cake
stood in the middle of the table decorated
all over with stars and bats and stripes.
Hundreds of candles were stuck into
the icing.

'That's a lot of candles!' said
Samantha.

'It's the way they do it at vampire and fairy parties,' I explained proudly.

Mum and Dad smiled down at me and then everyone started to sing.

'Happy birthday to you, happy birthday to you, happy biiiirthday, Isadoraaa . . .'

I tried hard to blow all the candles out. It took a long time and in the end everyone had to join in.

Dad started to cut the cake.

'This top layer is the red layer,' he said. 'Specially for vampires.' He handed a piece to Oliver.

'The second layer is for fairies,' said Mum. 'It's got flower petals in it and changes flavour whenever you take a bite.'

She cut a slice from the fairy layer and handed it to Samantha.

'The rest is regular human cake,' said Dad. 'Who wants a slice?'

Everyone put up their hands but no one wanted to eat the regular human sponge. They all wanted a slice of the fairy and vampire cakes.

'It's so yummy!' said Oliver.

'You'd better have some red juice to wash it down with,' said Dad,

 handing him a carton from the fridge.

'This has been the most exciting party ever!' said Zoe happily.

'I'm sad it's almost over,' said
Samantha.

'Well, you mustn't leave without
your party bags,' said Dad, hurrying out
to fetch them. He came back and handed
my friends one each.

'Ooh,' said Sashi pulling something
out of her bag. 'What's this?'

'It's a packet of seeds,' said Mum.
'To grow your own flowers with. Nature
is very important.'

'There's also some more cake in
there,' said Dad, 'wrapped in a tissue like
it's supposed to be.'

'I've got a pot of hair gel!'
yelled Bruno.

'I've got a flower crown,' said
Samantha.

'I've got some toothpaste in mine,'
said Oliver, puzzled.

'That's special toothpaste,' said Dad.
'It keeps your vampire fangs nice and
white. Very important!'

Oliver looked surprised. 'But my vampire fangs are just pretend ones!' he said. He put his hand to his mouth and pulled out a set of plastic fangs. Dad's eyes nearly popped out of his head.

'Wha . . . !?' he stuttered.

'I bought them from the costume shop,' said Oliver. 'They only cost fifty pence.'

'Fifty pence!' Dad gasped. 'The cheek!'

He was still recovering from his shock when the doorbell started to ring. It was time for my friends to go home.

Zoe was the last to leave.

'Goodbye, Isadora,' she said, giving

me a warm hug. 'Thank you for a lovely party!'

'Thank you for coming!' I said. And I meant it.

'Phew!' said Dad, leaning against the door when Zoe had disappeared down the front garden path with her mum. 'I'm exhausted!'

'Me too,' said Mum.

Wilbur slunk into the hallway.

'I'm leaving now too, Uncle and Auntie,' he said.

'Ah, Wilbur!' said Dad. 'I forgot you were still here. Thank you for your . . . help today.'

Wilbur looked a bit sheepish as he fiddled with his starry wizard hat.

'Ahem,' he said. 'That's quite all right.'

Then he looked at me.

'Sorry, Isadora,' he said gruffly.
'I should have listened to you more today.'

Then he scooted quickly out of the front door before I could say anything. I was shocked. Wilbur had just *apologized* to me!

I still felt stunned as I followed Mum and Dad back into the kitchen to unwrap my present. Mum opened the cupboard under the sink and took out the package from earlier. We all sat round the table.

'This is a very special present,' said Mum, handing it to me.

'But today you've proved you are definitely old enough to use it,' said Dad, smiling.

I started to unwrap the long thin package. What could it be?

'It's a . . . WAND!!!' I screamed, jumping off my chair and into the air. 'My very own wand! Thank you, thank you!' I said, dancing round the kitchen waving it so that sparks shot out of the star. 'It's the best present ever!'

Dad smiled and put
his arm round Mum. Mum
yawned and leaned her head
on Dad. They both closed
their eyes.

'We're glad you
like it,' they murmured
sleepily.

Pink Rabbit and I took
another slice of cake and
wandered back into the great
hall on our own. I waved my
new wand around, practising
using it on small things.
I changed the colours of the
balloons and made one of them

do a loop the loop in the air. Then I sat down next to the pile of presents from my friends.

'It was a fun party overall, wasn't it?' I said, licking the last of the icing off my fingers.

Pink Rabbit nodded.

'I mean, it got a bit tricky at some points,' I said. 'But I think everything turned out OK in the end. I think my friends enjoyed it. Don't you?'

Pink Rabbit nodded again and snuggled into me.

'It was very kind of Mum and Dad to organize such a nice party for me,' I said. 'I am glad they are the way they are. If they were any different then I wouldn't be me! And I love being a vampire fairy really.'

I pulled the first present on to my lap and started to unwrap it.

'I'm also glad my friends are the way

they are,' I continued. 'They are all very special too.'

Pink Rabbit smiled sleepily and yawned.

'I've had a great birthday,' I said. 'But even so . . . I think I will organize my own party next year!'

Isadora loves dressing up.
What's your favourite outfit?

Ballerina

Mermaid

Dinosaur

Ice cream

Princess

Witch

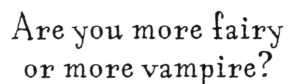

# Are you more fairy or more vampire?

## Take the quiz to find out!

### What's your favourite colour?

**A.** Pink    **B.** Black    **C.** I love them both!

### Would you rather go to:

**A.** A glittery school that teaches magic, ballet, and making flowery crowns?

**B.** A spooky school that teaches gliding, bat training, and how to have the sleekest hair possible?

**C.** A school where everyone gets to be totally different and interesting?

### On your camping holiday, do you:

**A.** Put up your tent with a wave of your magic wand and go exploring?

**B.** Pop up your fold-out four-poster bed and avoid the sun?

**C.** Splash about in the sea and have a great time?

# Results

## Mostly As
You are a glittery, dancing fairy and you love nature!

## Mostly Bs
You are a sleek, caped vampire and you love the night!

## Mostly Cs
You are half fairy, half vampire and totally unique – just like Isadora Moon!

# Isadora Moon

# Isadora Moon
# Goes to School

Her mum is a fairy and her dad is a vampire
and she is a bit of both. She loves the night, bats,
and her black tutu, but she also loves the sunshine,
her magic wand, and Pink Rabbit.

When it's time for Isadora to start school
she's not sure where she belongs—fairy school
or vampire school?

# Isadora Moon
# Goes Camping

It is the first day back at school after the summer, and Isadora is called on to talk about her holidays at show-and-tell. She's worried. She had been to the seaside, like her friends, but strange things had happened there ... the sort of things that probably didn't happen on human holidays.

# Isadora Moon
# Goes to the Ballet

Her mum is a fairy and her dad is a vampire
and she is a bit of both. Isadora loves ballet,
especially when she's wearing her black tutu,
and she can't wait to see a real show at the
theatre with the rest of her class.

But when the curtain rises,
where is Pink Rabbit?

Harriet Muncaster, that's me! I'm the author and illustrator of Isadora Moon. Yes really! I love anything teeny tiny, anything starry, and everything glittery.

# Love Isadora Moon?
## Why not try these too . . .

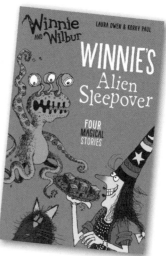